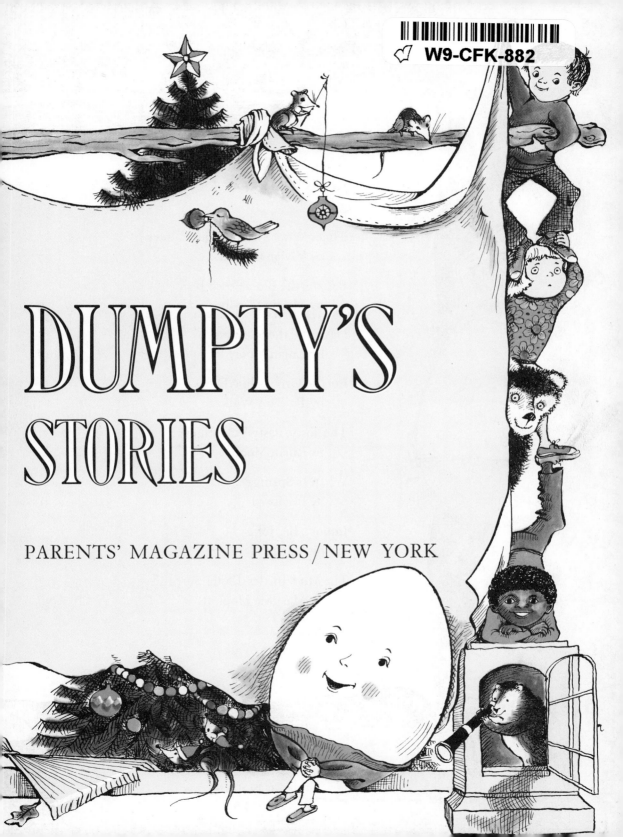

DUMPTY'S STORIES

PARENTS' MAGAZINE PRESS/NEW YORK

CONTENTS

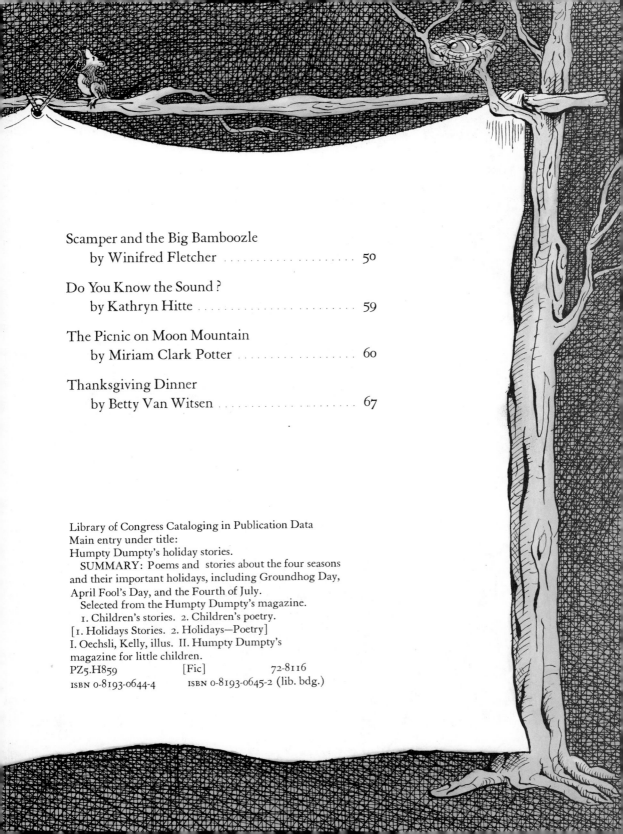

Library of Congress Cataloging in Publication Data
Main entry under title:
Humpty Dumpty's holiday stories.
    SUMMARY: Poems and stories about the four seasons
and their important holidays, including Groundhog Day,
April Fool's Day, and the Fourth of July.
    Selected from the Humpty Dumpty's magazine.
    1. Children's stories. 2. Children's poetry.
[1. Holidays Stories. 2. Holidays—Poetry]
I. Oechsli, Kelly, illus. II. Humpty Dumpty's
magazine for little children.
PZ5.H859   [Fic]   72-8116
ISBN 0-8193-0644-4   ISBN 0-8193-0645-2 (lib. bdg.)

THAT'S WHAT I LIKE ABOUT WINTER

BY VIVIAN GOULED

Flakes of snow that flurry by,
Making drifts that pile up high,
    That's what I like about winter!

Shiny ice that's new and hard,
Good for sliding in my yard,
    That's what I like about winter!

Going coasting on my sled,
Puffy covers on my bed,
    That's what I like about winter!

Feeding hungry little birds,
Happy Merry Christmas words,
    That's what I like about winter!

BASCOM THE BLUE-NOSED BEAR

BY MARTIN GARDNER

A light snow was gently falling over Mothergoose-land as Herman, the little elephant, trotted along the road with Junior riding on his back. Junior was wearing his stocking cap, mittens, and a heavy sweater under his coat, and Herman had on his woolen nose muff to keep his trunk from freezing.

Can you imagine why the two friends were out-of-doors on such a cold Saturday night? Well— it was Christmas Eve and they had decided to go from house to house and sing Christmas carols to their neighbors.

"Who shall we sing to next?" asked Herman. "I think we've been to every house in this block."

"All except one," Junior answered. "Let's not forget Bascom."

"Bascom!" snorted the elephant. "You mean that rich old bear with the blue nose who lives all by himself and hates everybody?"

"That's right," said Junior. "But I don't think he *really* hates everybody. I think he just pretends to. Anyway, maybe we can cheer him up if we sing to him."

"I doubt it," said Herman, shaking his head. "He doesn't like Christmas at all. He just stays inside his house and won't talk to anyone until Christmas is over. And even then all he ever says is 'Bah' and 'Humbug.'"

When they reached Bascom's house, Junior slid down from Herman's back and they walked through the snow until they were right in front of the door. Herman took off his nose muff so his voice would sound better; then they sang:

Silent night,
Holy night,
All is calm,
All is...

That was as far as they got, because the door opened suddenly and there stood Bascom. He was holding a pail of water.

"All is wet!" shouted the bear as he tossed the water at them. They jumped away just in time to keep from getting drenched.

"Too bad I missed," Bascom growled. "I hope this teaches you two whippersnappers not to come around my house at night and wake me up when I'm trying to get some sleep. Christmas carols indeed! Bah! Humbug!" He slammed the door with such a loud bang that it knocked several icicles off the edge of the roof.

"What did I tell you?" said Herman. "Why, I ought to fill my trunk with water and stick it through the window and squirt right in his face!"

"No, no," Junior said. "That would only make Bascom angrier. I've got a better idea." He bent over and whispered in Herman's ear, just in case the bear was listening behind the door. The elephant shook his head at first, but he finally agreed to do what Junior suggested. The little egg climbed on Herman's back and off they trotted through the falling snow.

When they returned to Bascom's house an hour later, Herman was carrying a large basket with his trunk. It was filled with jars of delicious honey. They had been singing Christmas carols around the neighborhood and at each house they had asked for a jar of honey to give to Bascom. In this way they had managed to collect more than twenty jars!

Junior and Herman tiptoed up to the house and left the basket in front of the door. "Merry Christmas!" they shouted. Then Junior hopped on Herman's back and the elephant trotted off as fast as he could.

A moment later the door opened. Bascom was holding a pail of water in his paw. He peered this way and that through the swirling snowflakes before he noticed the basket. He looked inside, picked it up and carried it into his house and closed the door.

The next day was Christmas, and Junior was so excited playing with the toys Santa had brought him that he almost forgot about Bascom. Then along about ten in the morning, the doorbell rang. Junior opened the front door and who do you suppose was standing there? It was Bascom—all dressed up in his best Sunday clothes and wearing a sprig of green and red holly in his lapel!

"Merry Christmas, everybody!" the bear called out, waving a paw toward Mr. and Mrs. Dumpty who were sitting in the living room. Then he handed Junior a shiny silver dollar. "I'm giving one of these to every boy and girl in Mothergooseland," he said with a chuckle. "I've got millions of 'em at home in a trunk and what good are dollars if you never use them?"

Before Junior could thank him, Bascom tipped his silk hat and walked away. In the distance the bells of the church began to ring out through the clear, frosty air. The bells were playing *Joy to the World* and Bascom smiled and hummed the tune to himself as he stepped briskly along.

"Good gracious!" exclaimed Mrs. Dumpty after Junior closed the door. "What in the world has happened to old Blue Nose?"

"Perhaps," said Junior thoughtfully, "somebody was nice to him for a change."

DAVY AND THE SNOW

BY LILIAN MOORE

Davy Brown was moving to a new home, far from the house he'd always lived in. He worried about it a lot. All the way there he thought, "Will I like it there? Will I like it in Hilltown so far away?"

The new street had tall trees, the new house had a big backyard, and Davy had an interesting time exploring inside and out.

"Well, Davy," his father asked, "how do you like your new home?"

"I think I like it," said Davy. "But why is it so cold here?"

"We are up in the north now," Davy's mother explained. "When we lived in the south it was always warm. But winter is cold in the north. And it's winter now in Hilltown."

The next morning Davy and his mother and his father—and his grandma and grandpa, too—ate their first breakfast in the new house.

"Davy thinks it's cold in Hilltown," said his mother.

"It will be even colder tonight," said Grandpa Brown. "Look at the sky. I think we are going to have some snow."

"Snow?" said Davy. "Tell me about snow."

"It's hard to explain," said his father. "Snow is, well, it's white. When the snow comes down, everything looks white."

"Yes, snow is white," said Davy's mother. "But snow is cold, too."

"That's right," said Grandpa Brown, "snow is white and cold. But it's wet, too. When you pick up snow, your hands get wet."

"Yes, Davy," said his grandma. "Snow is white and cold and wet. But snow is beautiful, too! It's soft to walk on and beautiful to look at."

The next morning Davy opened his eyes. He lay in bed, wondering.

Everything was strangely quiet. There were no morning sounds, no sounds of cars and traffic, no sounds of people coming and going.

He jumped out of bed and ran to the window. Then Davy just stood and stared at what he saw. The whole world looked different. Everything was white, the trees, the houses, the backyard. The snow had come down softly in the night, and covered it all.

"How white snow is!" thought Davy. He opened his window a little and put his hand out on the sill. For the very first time he touched snow.

"How cold snow is!" he thought. He looked at his hand. "It's wet, too!"

When Davy ran out to play that morning, he had more clothes on than he had ever worn at one time before. A warm hat and coat, warm mittens, a warm red sweater. And—best of all—shiny new black boots. Davy walked happily around in the new snow. Each time he put his foot down, he could see the print of his boot.

"I'm the very first one to walk on this snow," he said to himself. "Everywhere I walk here I'm the very first one!"

Then Davy picked up some snow and rolled it in his mittens. Why, it made a ball! He threw it at a tree, and watched it make a snowspatter. Then Davy made one snowball after another, throwing them at trees and fences.

Soon a boy with a red woolen cap and red mittens came by pulling a sled.

"Hi!" he called to Davy. "Want to ride on my sled?"

Davy got his first ride on a sled. First the boy pulled Davy on the sled and then Davy pulled the boy. They walked to the end of the street where there was a little hill. Again and again they sledded down the hill.

When they were tired of the sledding, they began to roll a big snowball down the hill. It grew bigger and bigger and bigger. Soon they had a great fat snowman. They gave him a silly face, and a silly hat, and then they took turns throwing snowballs at him.

Davy was astonished when it was time to go home.

That night, Davy said, "Why didn't you tell me what snow is like?"

"But Davy," said his father. "We did tell you!"

"Snow is white, isn't it?" said his mother.

"Snow is wet, isn't it?" asked his Grandpa.

"And isn't the snow beautiful, Davy?" said his Grandma.

"Oh, of course," said Davy. "But that isn't what snow is most of all!"

"Then what *is* snow, Davy?" asked his mother.

Davy thought of all the things he had done that day. "Why, it's to play in!" said Davy. "Most of all, snow is fun!"

FUN ON
GROUNDHOG DAY

BY BARBARA WALKER

There are shadows you make in the sunshine,
There are shadows you make by the lamp,
There are shadows that lurk in the forest
While you tell creepy stories at camp.

There are shadows that help you with puppets,
And shadows you make just for play,
But the shadow that's *famous* is Groundhog's,
When he tells whether winter's to stay.

Let's go out very early this morning
And watch for his shadow, my son;
It may not be at all scientific,
But you've got to admit that it's fun!

THE TASTY, PASTY VALENTINES

BY LILIAN MOORE

Little Gray Mouse looked around his cozy little home. "Oh, I am the lucky one!" he thought.

He *was* lucky. His little hole in the wall was just right. The house he lived in was just right, too.

People lived in the house, of course—a mother and a father, a boy and a girl. But Gray Mouse did not mind that. "They are nice, quiet people," Mouse told his friends. "They don't give me much trouble." And they did have a fine kitchen. A fellow could always pick up a little snack at bedtime.

Little Gray Mouse lived in a hole in the wall of the boy's room. That was lucky, too. For the boy left such *good* crumbs. Cake crumbs! Bread crumbs with peanut butter! Yum!

But sometimes the boy would stay in his room —right in Gray Mouse's way. That was the trouble right now. Mouse wanted to go down to the kitchen. He wanted to go very, very much, for he could smell—cheese! Lovely, lovely cheese! But the boy was in the room. So was the girl. They were sitting at the table, working.

"Why don't they go out to play?" Little Gray Mouse thought crossly.

But the boy and girl went on working. They had red paper and white paste and scissors. Snip! Snip! They cut up the red paper. Swoosh! Swoosh! Swoosh! They put paste on the red paper, here and there.

"Oh dear!" said the girl. "Something's wrong. The ones I make look funny."

"Mine look kind of funny, too," said the boy. "I can't make them look right."

The girl looked as if she wanted to cry. "Oh dear!" she said again. "I especially wanted them to look pretty."

"Well, let's get them done anyway," said the boy. "Then we can go out and play."

"Yes, indeed!" thought Little Gray Mouse. "Do get done! Do go away!" How he did want to get to that cheese!

At last the boy and girl stood up. They put the red papers on the floor.

"I wish they looked better," said the girl.

"Come on," said the boy. "They'll dry soon. Maybe they will look better then." And they ran out to play.

Little Gray Mouse popped out of his hole. He was about to scamper down to the kitchen. Suddenly he stopped. Sniff! Sniff! What a wonderful smell! Sniff! Sniff! Why, it came from the red papers on the floor! It was the wonderful smell of white paste!

Little Gray Mouse ran to the red papers and began to nibble at them. Nibble! Nibble! Nibble! Delicious! He nibbled all around the red papers, in and out and around and around. Nibble, nibble, he went, wherever there was that wonderful taste of paste. "Best meal I've had around here in a long time," he said happily.

Soon he was so full that he did not even go down to the kitchen. Instead, he went back to his cozy little mouse house for a good after-nibble nap.

Little Gray Mouse was still sleeping when the boy and girl returned. They ran into the room. Then they stopped in astonishment.

"Look at our valentines!" cried the boy.

"Why, they're beautiful!" cried the girl. She jumped up and down and clapped her hands.

"I wonder who did this for us?" said the boy. "They look as if they have been nibbled." Nibbled! The boy and girl looked at each other and began to laugh.

"I know who it was!" said the boy.

"So do I," said the girl. "And we must say Thank you!"

Soon after that, Little Gray Mouse woke up from his nap. Something wonderful woke him in the middle of a dream. Sniff! Sniff! He had never smelled anything so good before—and it came from the boy's room.

Gray Mouse ran out of his hole as fast as he could. "What's this?" said the mouse in surprise.

There in the middle of the room was some red paper.

There in the middle of the red paper was a piece of cheese. And there on the cheese was some paste!

There were words on the red paper. They said
Be Our Valentine!

But Little Gray Mouse didn't care about
words. Cheese and paste! It's not often that you
can eat cheese and paste at the same time!

"What a day!" he said happily. "What a lovely,
lovely day!"

WHEN IS SPRING?

BY BEE LEWI

You ask me how you'll know it's spring.
It isn't dates or days.
Spring is magic that you feel
In special, secret ways.

A bird you heard just yesterday
Now sings a sweeter call.
The grass is shining extra green,
And softer raindrops fall.

A leaf that blows across your cheek
Is like a velvet wing.
You sniff the air, and suddenly
You tell yourself, "It's spring!"

JUNIOR'S BIG JOKE

BY MARTIN GARDNER

When Mrs. Dumpty walked into the bathroom she
saw a strange sight. Junior was standing on a chair
in front of the washbasin, with a paintbrush in one
hand and a box of watercolors in the other. He
was leaning forward so he could see his face up
close in the mirror, and he was painting a huge
black mustache under his nose.

"What in the world are you doing?" Mrs. Dumpty asked. "I hope you haven't forgotten that you have to get a haircut today."

"I haven't forgotten," Junior said. "Today is April Fools' Day and I'm going to play a funny joke on Mr. Shaggy the barber. You know how nearsighted he is."

Mrs. Dumpty nodded. "That's because he's a sheep dog. It's hard for him to see through all that hair that covers his eyes."

"He never recognizes me until he comes over to cut my hair," Junior continued. "So I'm going to pretend I'm a grown-up man and want to have my mustache trimmed. Won't he be surprised when he finds out it's just me?"

"He will indeed," said Mrs. Dumpty, who couldn't help smiling at Junior's plans.

When Junior finished painting on his mustache, he put away his paints, then hurried down the stairs and out the door. It was only a short walk to Mr. Shaggy's barbershop. When he entered,

Mr. Shaggy was wringing out a wet towel in a small white pan that he kept on a shelf at the back of the shop.

Junior slipped into the barber's chair. Then he called out in a deep, gruff voice, "I'd like to have my mustache trimmed, please!"

The barber raised his head and squinted at Junior through the shaggy hair that hung down over his eyes. "I beg your pardon," he said. "I didn't see you come in." He picked up his scissors and walked over to the chair.

"That's a handsome mustache you have there," he commented.

"Thank you," Junior replied. "Please trim it a bit, but not *too* much, because I like to have it long enough to curl up at the ends."

"I understand, sir," said Mr. Shaggy. He bent over and started to clip the mustache. But there was nothing to clip! The ends of his scissors just slid over the white shell of the little egg's upper lip!

Mr. Shaggy was very much surprised. He lifted

up the hair that hung over one eye so he could get a better look. "Why," he exclaimed, "it's Humpty Dumpty Junior!"

Junior laughed out loud. "April Fool!" he shouted.

The barber put his hands on his hips and

smiled. "Well, I must say you certainly fooled me good. I guess you really came here for a haircut, didn't you?"

Junior was still laughing too hard to talk. He just nodded his head while Mr. Shaggy fastened the sheet around his neck. When the barber started to cut his hair, Junior closed his eyes. It was warm inside the shop and after a few minutes the little egg fell fast asleep.

Ten minutes later Junior felt someone shaking his shoulder. "Wake up, my boy!" the barber said. "Your haircut's finished. How do you like it?"

Junior opened his eyes sleepily and glanced at his reflection in the mirror. Suddenly his eyes opened wide! His head was completely bald!

"April Fool!" Mr. Shaggy called out.

Junior jumped out of the chair and felt the top of his head. It was as smooth as the end of an egg! "Oh! Oh!" he wailed. "What a terrible thing to do! You've cut off all my hair!"

Before the barber could answer, Junior turned and ran out of the shop. The sheet was still tied around his neck and it flapped behind him as he ran. He ran all the way home.

"Mother!" he cried. "Come and see what Mr. Shaggy did to me!"

Mrs. Dumpty rushed into the living room and threw up her hands in horror. Then suddenly she started to laugh.

"I don't think it's funny at all," Junior said, frowning.

His mother walked over and put her hands on each side of Junior's head. Then she lifted. Off came the white enamel pan that Mr. Shaggy used for soaking his towels!

"It's just one of Mr. Shaggy's shaggy-dog jokes," she said. "He put his pan upside-down on your head to make it look as though you were bald. As a matter of fact he gave you a *very* neat haircut."

Junior stared at the pan. He reached up and felt his hair. Then he grinned from ear to ear. "Well, what do you think of that!" he exclaimed. "I'll take the pan back to Mr. Shaggy right now and apologize. I guess it serves me right for the April Fool joke I played on him!"

THE MUD TURTLES' EASTER SURPRISE

BY MARJORIE HOPKINS

It was very early in the morning, already too light for Mr. Owl to be out. But he was having such a good time sailing his new red boat that he kept gliding on down Clear Stream. Along the low river bank ran a path with daisies bobbing along its edge.

Suddenly Mr. Owl saw a basket on the path near Mrs. Rabbit's house.

"That's a basket of eggs, as sure as tomorrow's Easter," said Mr. Owl. "Mrs. Rabbit has put them there, hoping somebody will take them to Forest Deeps for the egg hunt. I can take them for her in my boat."

Mr. Owl steered the boat toward the bank. He stretched out his wing and lifted the basket aboard. Some of the eggs were pink with red dots, some were golden yellow all over, and some had purple stripes. They were shiny with the wax that Mrs. Rabbit rubbed on to protect the colors.

Mr. Owl set the basket on the middle seat of the boat. Then on down the stream he sailed. He sang softly to himself, for he was very musical.

> *An Easter egg is good to see,*
> *It's just as nice to feel.*
> *It's smooth as sailing, bright as dawn,*
> *And lots of fun to peel.*

Even though he sang, Mr. Owl watched for sticks and stones that might upset his boat. He got along fine for a while; then it got harder and harder for him to see as the day grew brighter.

"Why, I can hardly read that sign," he said, squinting his eyes to peer at a paper tacked to a post on the bank. He sailed near the bank again, and squinted his eyes still more as he read:

GONE TU GET NEW STRINGS
ON OUR GEETARS. BAK SUN.
THE MUD TERTLES

Mr. Owl knew by this that he was sailing past the Mud Turtles' home. They were a lazy lot, the Mud Turtles. They just lay around in the sun, or they swam in the muddy shallows, idly strumming their guitars. The other animals didn't pay much attention to them.

Mr. Owl tried to get his boat out into the middle of the stream again. But he didn't see the broad log the Mud Turtles sunned themselves on. The boat ran into it and nearly tipped over. Before Mr. Owl could get it straight again, the basket of eggs slid neatly over the side and the eggs settled on the mud below!

"I shouldn't try to sail in the daylight," Mr. Owl scolded himself. The basket floated to the top of the water. Mr. Owl rescued it, then pulled the boat to shore between the sign and the willow tree. He decided to rest under the tree until the Mud Turtles returned and got the eggs out of the water for him. They still looked as pretty as ever, though they rested on the bed of Clear Stream.

Mr. Owl had barely settled himself when he felt a soft paw touch his wing.

It was Dilly Fox, with a bouquet of daisies and buttercups in one paw.

"Hello, Dilly," said Mr. Owl.

"Hello, Mr. Owl! What's going to go into your basket?" asked Dilly, who looked very nice in her new pink Easter dress.

GONE TO GET NEW STRINGS ON OUR GEETARS. BAK SUN. THE MUD TURT

"Eggs, I hope." Mr. Owl blinked, pointing to the eggs in the stream. At least, he *thought* they were there. He could hardly see. "I'm waiting for the Mud Turtles to get home and rescue them for me. I was taking them to Forest Deeps for Mrs. Rabbit."

"Oh, my!" said Dilly. "Mrs. Rabbit *never* gives Easter eggs to the Mud Turtles. She tells her friends they aren't worth the shells they live under. They make impolite remarks to her when she passes by on the path with her Easter eggs."

"I don't steer very well when it's light," Mr. Owl apologized. "My boat hit the Mud Turtles' log. I didn't see it."

"But how can we be sure the Mud Turtles will give them back?" said Dilly, sitting down by Mr. Owl.

Before Mr. Owl could answer, old Timothy Mud Turtle's wrinkled head rose slowly out of the ripples at their feet.

"Howdy, folks!" he said. "We just got back from gettin' our geetars fixed and found the nicest surprise! You and Mrs. Rabbit are most uncommon kind to us!"

"He thinks you left the eggs there—on purpose!" Dilly whispered to Mr. Owl.

Mr. Owl squeezed Dilly's paw gently with his wing.

"You're welcome, I'm sure," he told Timothy with old-world charm.

Timothy turned and slipped back into the water. Almost at once he returned with a small guitar in one hand.

"You like to have my geetar?" he asked Mr. Owl shyly. "I don't play nearly as well as the rest of my family. You're welcome to it. Now I'm goin' down and admire those pretty eggs some more."

45

And not waiting for Mr. Owl or Dilly to say a word, he laid the guitar on the bank and slipped away again. The water became muddy, and Mr. Owl knew the whole Mud Turtle family was admiring the eggs.

"That is nice, having a guitar!" said Mr. Owl. "I used to play one when I was an owlet. Did he *really* leave me a guitar?"

All Mr. Owl could see on the bank was a brownish blur.

"Yes, Mr. Owl!" said Dilly. She ran and got the guitar for him.

"I suppose I shouldn't sail till it gets dark," said Mr. Owl. "But I would love to play and sing while I sail! I can't wait!"

"The river's deeper and wider now, all the way to Clear Cove," said Dilly, as Mr. Owl fumbled his way into the boat, with the guitar under one wing. "I'll take the basket to Mrs. Rabbit and tell her what happened. I'm glad the Mud Turtles got the eggs. They're probably all as happy about them as Timothy is. They'll never bother Mrs. Rabbit again when she passes by."

"I think you're right," said Mr. Owl, settling himself with his guitar. "Happy Easter, Dilly! Good-by!"

Down the stream he sailed, and as he sailed he strummed the guitar and sang:

> *A turtle may be gruff and rough*
> *And know not how to spell,*
> *But he hides a heart of gold*
> *Beneath a muddy shell!*

SUMMER

BY BARBARA WALKER

Can you guess where Junior is?
He's hiding in the grass,
Waiting very quietly
To watch a beetle pass.

48

Can you guess what Junior's hearing?
    It's the cricket's song,
One of many special noises
    Summer brings along.

Can you think what Junior's sniffing?
    It's a yellow rose;
Such a lemon-yellow flavor
    Sits upon his nose!

Mom, why don't *we* dry the dishes,
    Though they're Junior's chore—
He's so busy *feeling summer,*
    And that's what summer's for!

SCAMPER AND THE BIG BAMBOOZLE

BY WINIFRED FLETCHER

Scamper Soon sat under the Bamboozle Bush with his friends Skip and Tootle-oo, making wishes.

"I wish today was my birthday," Scamper said.

"It soon will be," Skip answered. "Next month."

"Soon! Soon!" Scamper said. "Everything will be 'soon'—my birthday, the circus, Fourth of July. Why can't they be *now?* Even my name is Soon!"

"Yes, your father's Mighty Soon."

"And your mother's Pretty Soon," laughed Tootle-oo.

Just then a leaf fell on Scamper's neck.

"You're lucky!" Skip cried. "That leaf's a Boozle. The Bamboozle Bush sheds its leaves only once in ten years but if one falls on you, you can wish anything you please and it will come true!"

"Whoopee! I wish," Scamper said, loud and clear, "that my birthday and the circus and the Fourth of July would all come at once—right *now!*"

For a moment, nothing happened. Then his mother called, "Come here, Scamper!"

Under the apple tree, his friends were seated around a table.

"It's your party!" Tootle-oo exclaimed.

"It's the Fourth!" Skip said. "Hear the band?"

Just then a big steam calliope blared up the drive.

"Circus, circus!" the children yelled. "See the elephants!"

An elephant, big as a house, swayed toward Scamper. Its ears flapped like pancakes; then its trunk curled itself *right around Scamper* and lifted him up, up in the air. The elephant waved Scamper back and forth gently. At first it was fun, but as he went higher and higher, an elevatorish feeling began in his stomach.

"Put me down!" he begged.

And that elephant set Scamper in the big apple tree, right over the birthday table!

Scamper slid down and his mother caught him.

The children crowded around, laying their gifts on the table. "Happy Birthday!" they sang.

But when Scamper started to open the presents, a cute little monkey grabbed one package and unwrapped a big red truck. Then he got inside the truck and tried to run it.

Everybody laughed. But before Scamper could open the other presents, a circus man called, "Come see the show—just starting!"

Away they went to a big tent to see the trapeze acts.

As they reached the tent, it began to get dark and someone yelled, "The fireworks are beginning at the pool!"

Scamper stopped. If he saw the circus, he'd miss the fireworks. He *must* see *them*. He walked toward the pool and the first Roman candle exploded in a shower of sparks.

His mother called, "Come, the ice cream's ready!"

Scamper paused. His birthday party—he *couldn't* miss *that!*

But just then a sky rocket whooshed off, and twelve pinwheels made dazzling circles. Two tinsel-dressed ladies turning somersaults on white horses galloped by.

"Come to the tent!" Skip yelled. "The lions are doing tricks!"

"I've *got* to see *them!*" Scamper cried.

But that minute, the American flag in fire-works appeared over the pool. Scamper saluted while the colors of Old Glory lit the sky, reflected in the water.

When they faded, he ran to the tent.

Skip met him. "The acts are all over."

"Oh dear!" Scamper grumbled. "Why does everything have to come all at once?"

"That's what you wished for," Tootle-oo told him.

"Scamper, come now!" His mother was almost crying. "Your party'll be ruined!"

Scamper hurried to the table.

"Happy birthday!" they sang again. But the calliope drowned them out. The circus was leaving. The band blared, men shouted, people blew squawkers. Lions roared, horses whinnied, as the wagons rumbled off.

The noise made Scamper's head ache.

At last they were gone. "*Now* we can have the party."

"Everything's spoiled," his mother said sadly. The tablecloth was torn, the gifts were gone, and the ice cream stood in little pink pools in each dish.

"You stayed away so long, it all melted," Skip said. "And the monkeys ate the candy and took the presents."

"They popped the poppers, too," giggled Tootle-oo. "It was funny."

It didn't seem funny to Scamper. "I'm sorry," he said to his mother. He began to eat the warm, gooey ice cream.

Then Mrs. Pretty Soon uncovered the most beautiful birthday cake he'd ever seen. On top was a sparkly sugar space rocket, and there were eight red candles.

Scamper beamed. "That's swell, Mom!"

She lit the candles and he leaned over to blow them out, when a strange thing happened. The candles exploded. *Bang! Bang! Bang!*

Scamper nearly jumped out of his skin. His eyes stung, he tasted powder, his tongue smarted. They weren't candles at all—they were *small firecrackers!* The cake was a wreck. Bits of red paper stuck in the frosting.

"That's what comes of mixing circuses and Fourth of July and birthdays," Tootle-oo said.

Mrs. Soon looked shocked. "I thought they were candles. They looked so pretty."

Scamper felt sick. "It's not your fault, it's mine. I'm sorry I made that wish!" he cried. "Oh Mother, I'm sorry!"

Suddenly he grew dizzy. The children, the cake—seemed to melt away.

The next thing he knew, he was on the ground, rubbing his eyes, and the Boozle was tickling his nose. No, it *wasn't* a Boozle—just a leaf from the lilac bush. Skip and Tootle-oo were gone, and it was getting dark. His mother was calling, "Supper!"

"Supper?" said Scamper to himself. But what happened to the birthday party and the circus and the Fourth of July?

Then he laughed. "I don't care what happened to them," he said. "I just don't want them all to come at the same time ever again!" And he ran in to wash his hands.

DO YOU KNOW THE SOUND?

BY KATHRYN HITTE

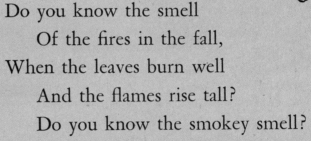

Do you know the sound
    Of the leaves in the fall
On the trees, on the ground,
    Or piled by the wall?
    Do you know the scuffly sound?

    Do you know the smell
        Of the fires in the fall,
    When the leaves burn well
        And the flames rise tall?
        Do you know the smokey smell?

Do you know the air
    That is best of all—
Crispy and clear and sharp and rare,
    The *feel* of the fall?
    Do you know that lovely spice-y
        Autumn-y air?
Do you know the fall?

THE PICNIC ON MOON MOUNTAIN

BY MIRIAM CLARK POTTER

Once there was a witch named Fly-by-Night. She had a big black cat for a pet. She used to look forward to Halloween, because then she flew around on a broomstick with her cat behind her. It was great fun.

Now Halloween was coming soon, and Fly-by-Night was planning what to do.

"I think," she said to her cat, "that we'll go as far toward the moon as we can. It's very cold up there; we don't want to go too high. Then, we'll swoop and see if we can shake the stars, and if we run across a comet we'll pull its tail. Won't that be nice?"

"No," grumbled her cat. "I don't think it will be nice at all. You drive too fast. I suppose we've got to go out on Halloween, for that's the rule. But I'd rather take a lunch and have a quiet picnic on a mountain top. I don't like speed, and you speed, you know you do! I have to hang on to the broomstick with all my claws."

"Oh," laughed the witch, "I can hardly wait! It's a pity we don't get a chance to fly except on Halloween. By the way, I wonder if our broomstick is in good order. It may need oiling."

She ran to check.

"It seems fine," she said happily. "But I'll put an extra splash of oil on just before we start, to make sure we swoosh."

The cat sat looking cross. "I don't want to swoosh," he said.

"Oh, you are a regular old Footstool," said Fly-by-Night. "I've often told you that. Well, I'll make a bargain with you. If you sit behind me quietly and don't growl, we'll have a picnic lunch when we get through riding and swooping. We'll take some catnip sandwiches and a bottle of goat's milk."

The cat looked pleased, and gave a sound that was half-growl, half-purr.

Halloween came; there was a big, bright moon. The witch and the cat got on the broomstick with the picnic basket. They rose, they swooped. They had to be careful not to bump into the other witches and cats flying around. The air seemed full of them!

After a while the cat asked, "Haven't we had enough? Can't we have our picnic now?"

"Oh, all right," said Fly-by-Night, and they came down on the craggy top of Moon Mountain.

They were settling themselves on a big stone to eat, when another witch and cat swooped above them. They came down and landed on a nearby stone.

"What *are* you doing?" asked the other witch.

"This is a picnic," said Fly-by-Night. "I didn't want one, but my cat hates riding around, and I am doing this just to please him."

"What a fine idea," said the other witch. "And it's very funny, but *my* cat, Bouncey-Ball, loves swooping and riding, but I don't. That's why he named me Stay-at-Home. And that's where I'd rather be, right now! But he makes me fly around on Halloween. He says that's what cats and witches are supposed to do. What's your name, by the way?"

"Fly-by-Night. And my cat is Footstool."

All this time Stay-at-Home and Bouncey-Ball had been staring at the good-looking picnic lunch. Fly-by-Night noticed this. She asked, "Will you have some lunch with us?"

"That will be lovely, thank you," said Stay-at-Home.

They settled themselves to eat, and Fly-by-Night said, "It's too bad you don't like to swoop and ride, Stay-at-Home."

"And it's too bad I don't, either," said Footstool.

Then Stay-at-Home's cat, Bouncey-Ball, spoke up. "I have an idea. Why can't I be your cat, Witch Fly-by-Night? And why can't your cat, Footstool, belong to my Stay-at-Home? Then we'd each suit the other."

"I wouldn't even have to go out on Halloween," said Stay-at-Home. "There'd be no restless cat to push me into it. I could stay by the fire with you, Footstool."

"And I could swoop with you, Bouncey," laughed Fly-by-Night. "There'd be no lazy cat behind me. I could speed!"

The witches and the cats all looked pleased.

When the picnic on Moon Mountain was over, Stay-at-Home and Footstool went right back to earth again.

But Fly-by-Night and Bouncey-Ball did more extra-fancy flying. They stayed out almost until dawn, and were the very last ones to leave the sky.

THANKSGIVING DINNER

BY BETTY VAN WITSEN

It was Thanksgiving Day. The whole family—all the relatives—Grandma and Grandpa, Aunt Ellie, Cousin Laura, Aunt Sara, and Uncle Stan were coming for dinner.

The soup was steaming on the stove.

The crackly brown turkey was hot on the platter.

The orange sweet potatoes were keeping warm in the oven.

The onions and the green peas and the long white parsnips were bubbling in their pots.

The pumpkin pie and the apple pie were cooling on the windowsill.

Daddy and Sadie were just tasting the cider, to be sure it was cold enough, and Mommy was just putting gravy in the gravy boat when the doorbell rang.

"I'll answer it!" said Sadie.

"Hi!" she said a minute later when she opened the door.

Everybody was there.

Aunt Ellie came in, her arms full of packages.

"Hi, sweet potato!" She grinned.

Sadie looked at her in surprise. "Oh, I'm not the sweet potato," said Sadie. "The sweet potatoes are baking in the oven. Come on into the kitchen, I'll show you."

They all followed Sadie into the kitchen.

"How are you, pumpkin?" Grandpa hugged her.

"No, I'm not the pumpkin, either," said Sadie. "The pumpkin's in the pie on the windowsill. Sweet potatoes in the oven, pumpkin pie on the windowsill."

"Hey, there, honey," Grandma murmured as she kissed her.

"No, I'm not honey," squeaked Sadie. The honey's in the apple pie! Sweet potatoes in the oven, pumpkin pie on the windowsill, honey in the apple pie—right there!" She pointed.

"Come give us a kiss, duck," coaxed tiny old Cousin Laura, holding out her arms.

"I'm not a duck!" cried Sadie. "No duck today. We're having TURKEY. There!" She pointed again. "Sweet potatoes in the oven, pumpkin pie on the windowsill, honey in the apple pie, and turkey on the platter."

"What do you say, sugar?" laughed fat Aunt Sara, wobbling her chins.

"Im NOT SUGAR!" yelled Sadie. The sugar's in the sugar bowl. Listen! Sweet potatoes in the oven, pumpkin pie on the windowsill, honey in the apple pie, turkey on the platter, and sugar in the sugar bowl. See!"

"Come sit on my lap, giblet," chuckled Uncle Stan, peeking over his glasses.

"I'm not a giblet." Sadie giggled. "The giblets